The House of Stairs

BARBARA VINE

Level 4

Retold by Stephen Waller
Series Editors: Andy Hopkins and Jocelyn Potter

Pearson Education Limited

Edinburgh Gate, Harlow,

Essex CM20 2JE, England

and Associated Companies throughout the world.

ISBN: 978-1-4058-8222-4

Typeset by Graphicraft Ltd, Hong Kong

Set in 11/14pt Bembo

Printed in China

SWTC/02

Published by Pearson Education Ltd in association with
Penguin Books Ltd, both companies being subsidiaries of Pearson Plc

For a complete list of the titles available in the Penguin Readers series please write to your local
Pearson Longman office or to: Penguin Readers Marketing Department, Pearson Education,
Edinburgh Gate, Harlow, Essex CM20 2JE, England.

Contents

Introduction

I remembered the first time I saw Bell, when she walked into the hall at Thornham and told us her husband had shot himself.

Bell Sanger is a strange and beautiful young woman – and she is a mystery.

Elizabeth is living in a friend's house in Notting Hill in London when she meets Bell for the second time. The house is tall and narrow and the people there call it the House of Stairs. Bell comes to live there, and complicated relationships begin to form.

Bell is healthy and intelligent, but she has no friends and no job. She never wants to work. No one knows where she is from, what she wants or where she is going.

As the truth is slowly uncovered, it is far worse than anyone imagined. Is it too late to stop the secrets of the past from damaging everyone's lives?

Barbara Vine's real name is Ruth Rendell, and she is one of Britain's best-selling crime writers. People who love crime fiction call her the Queen of Crime.

Rendell was born in London in 1930. Her parents, an English father and a Swedish mother, were both teachers in East London. The family spent many holidays in Scandinavia, where Ruth learnt to speak Swedish and Danish. Her parents had a terrible marriage, often shouting at each other and arguing. Ruth had a difficult childhood but has always refused to talk about it in interviews. Her mother was ill, but nobody knew for years. She often fell over and dropped things. The doctors did not discover her illness until Ruth was nearly twenty.

Ruth's first job was as a journalist on a local newspaper. She was told to write about the local Tennis Club dinner. She wrote her story before the dinner, didn't go to the dinner and sent it in. So when the after-dinner speaker died during his speech, she didn't know about it. She left her job the next morning before they sacked her. But she married the boss! His name was Don Rendell and they had one child, a son, when Rendell was twenty.

Her first novel, *From Doon With Death*, came out when she was 34. This story introduced her famous and popular character, Chief Inspector Wexford. He has appeared in more than twenty novels since then. The Wexford stories take place in a fictional English town called Kingsmarkham. Her detective is an ordinary man who sometimes gets things wrong.

As well as her Wexford novels, she has written many other crime novels, several collections of short stories, and her Barbara Vine novels. Her most famous books include *The Lake of Darkness* (1980), *The Killing Doll* (1984), *The Tree of Hands* (1984), *Live Flesh* (1986), which the Spanish film-maker Pedro Almodóvar has filmed, *The Water's Lovely* (2006) and *Not in the Flesh* (2007).

Rendell first used the name Barbara Vine in 1985 for a story called *A Dark-Adapted Eye*. This book won the Mystery Writers of America's Edgar Allan Poe Award. 'Barbara' is her middle name and 'Vine' was her grandmother's surname.

Her Barbara Vine stories are different from her crime and Wexford stories. They are darker and move more slowly, and they usually take place in cities. Her characters are often affected by long shadows from the past, as Bell Sanger is in *The House of Stairs*. Often they begin with a family illness. In *The House of Stairs*, there is Huntington's disease in Elizabeth's family. The endings are often open: the murder or crime may be solved, but the guilty person is not always punished. Rendell writes about why people feel guilty and their reasons for murder and other crimes. She never describes violence and says she doesn't want to read about it. She examines her characters like a scientist.

Rendell has strong political opinions, and social questions are important in all her work. She is a member of the House of Lords, a part of the British government, and she works there every day.

She never eats meat and hates being late. She always wakes up very early and takes exercise, before spending the morning at her desk. She writes for four hours each day and never runs out of ideas for stories. She reads a lot, and her favourite books include J. D. Salinger's *Catcher in the Rye*, Harper Lee's *To Kill a Mockingbird* and *The Good Soldier* by Ford Madox Ford.

Ruth Rendell and P. D. James, Britain's other most famous crime writer, have changed crime writing. They have changed the question from 'Who did it?' to 'Why did they do it?'

Ruth Rendell wrote *The House of Stairs* in 1989. The story jumps backwards and forwards in time to different points in the story-teller's life. It's important to notice the time words and phrases when you're reading, so that you know which part of the story you are in. At the beginning of the story, the story-teller is about forty. She quickly goes back twenty years, to the first time she saw the House of Stairs. And then back to when she was fourteen, when her parents first told her a secret about herself.

We know from the beginning that Bell has been in prison, but we do not discover her crime until nearly the end of the book. Rendell gives us a lot of information during the story, but we do not know until the end what is important and what is not important. A lot of the details make better sense if you read the book a second time.

Bell was crossing the street in front of us. I almost shouted to the taxi-driver to stop.

Chapter 1   A Woman I Used to Know

The traffic-lights were changing from red to green when I saw her. She was crossing the street in front of us. I almost shouted to the taxi-driver to stop.

'I saw a woman I know, a woman I used to know. I have to talk to her,' I explained.

Bell was already disappearing among the crowds on their way home from work. But I was sure it was her. I had to follow her even after all these years and after all the terrible things.

I waited impatiently while the London traffic streamed past. A red wall of buses hid her from me, then I saw her again, tall and thin, dressed all in black. I noticed something different, though: her hair had changed colour. With a shock I realized that Bell's hair was grey.

The traffic-lights changed again and I went after her. It was sunset and the sky was red, with heavy, dark clouds. I looked along the Bayswater Road in both directions, but I couldn't see Bell. Perhaps she had walked up Queensway. Then I saw her again in the distance. Her grey hair was arranged on top of her head in the same way Cosette used to have her hair when she first came to the House of Stairs. I hadn't realized that Bell would be free already; another year at least, I had thought. I wondered, for the first time, would Bell want to see me? I couldn't imagine that she blamed me the way Cosette had blamed me. But did she think I blamed *her*? I hurried on, up St Petersburgh Place, along Moscow Road and into Pembridge Square, until finally I knew I had lost her. The sky wasn't red any longer, but a wild, stormy grey.

Of course I was in Notting Hill now, near the Portobello Road. There weren't many people in the streets. It had been different when I first came here nearly twenty years ago. The streets had been alive with young people then, wearing long hair and strange clothes, listening to loud music, enjoying a new freedom.

I started to walk back, but not the way I had come. I can't pretend I didn't know that those streets would lead me to Archangel Place. As I walked I thought of Bell. How could I find her? Had she seen me and wanted to hide? I had walked a lot and my legs began to hurt.

It is always the same, the feeling that this may be it, that this is not an ordinary tiredness but the early warning itself. The usual fear rushed through me. I am not old enough yet to be out of danger. I have never told anybody except Bell and Cosette. Well, naturally, Cosette knew already. Does Bell remember? I told myself, as usual, your legs hurt because you don't take any exercise.

Then I came to Archangel Place. I looked down the narrow, short street. At that distance the House of Stairs appeared unchanged. It was getting dark now. Slowly I walked down on the opposite side. On summer evenings when Cosette lived there, people used to sit outside talking and laughing. But Archangel Place has changed. The houses have become modern flats now, and the same thing has happened to the House of Stairs. Someone has changed the front door, but the front garden is the same. Although I couldn't see it, I knew that the back garden would be different. The new owners had obviously been told. I felt sure they had changed things to chase away the awful memory.

As I stood there, the central window on the first floor opened and I saw that Cosette's enormous living-room was now separated into smaller rooms. It was a shock, and in my mind I suddenly saw Cosette sitting at her table in that big room, smiling at me with her arms open wide.

As I was leaving Archangel Place, a taxi passed and I got into it. My thoughts returned to Bell. I knew now that I would find her. I thought sadly of her years in prison, the waste of life. Then I remembered the first time I saw Bell, when she walked into the hall at Thornham and told us her husband had shot himself.

Chapter 2   Inheritance

I was fourteen when they told me. My mother's illness was still hidden, but they had decided to tell me. Of course they knew it would frighten me and make me unhappy. But I was angry. If they knew the facts, why was I born at all? I told Bell one day in the House of Stairs, but I have never told anybody else. They were my parents, but for a time I didn't want to be their daughter. My mother fell ill, but I was still angry. I turned away from them to somebody who was kind and didn't cause me pain. I turned to Cosette.

I had known Cosette all my life. She was married to my mother's cousin Douglas Kingsley and lived quite near to us in a large house in Hampstead. Douglas was a rich businessman. Cosette and Douglas had the style of life which is typical of a certain class of rich people. I thought this lifestyle was something they both wanted and had chosen. Later I began to understand that Douglas had chosen it, not Cosette.

I began going to see her in those summer holidays after my parents told me of my inheritance. I was a child still, but she talked to me as if I was an adult, a friend. She knew my parents had told me and thought she could help. Cosette was like that. She welcomed me into her home. We sat in the garden and she talked to me about her plants. She knew all their names, but I never saw her do any work in the garden. She had a gardener for that. In fact she didn't seem to work at all. She was very good at doing nothing and liked to sit for hours, not reading or writing, just sitting. In those days she was a little older than I am now, a little over forty. To me she seemed extremely old. She was then a large fair woman, quite fat, with greyish-blue eyes. I soon began visiting her more often.

Cosette didn't ask me about the thing my parents had told me; she was waiting for me to start talking. When at last I decided to speak, I told her I would never have children. I guessed that she had never had children because of Douglas and his inheritance.

In the spring I spent most of my days with Cosette. Although she was almost thirty years older than me, I enjoyed being with her. I had made Cosette into another mother for myself. And in those days she didn't seem unhappy when people in shops and restaurants thought she was my mother. She didn't seem to worry about her age then. Later, in Archangel Place, that changed. But at that time, when I was fifteen, she didn't try to appear younger than she really was. She dressed in unattractive suits which made her look even older.

Years passed. As I grew older, although I always loved her, I began to dislike her appearance. Sometimes, when I took my friend Elsa with me to Cosette's house, we secretly laughed at her untidy hair and ugly clothes. It was cruel and it is painful for me now to remember, but I am trying to be completely honest. Quite often she took us into her bedroom and let us try on her expensive clothes and jewellery. That is when I first saw the bloodstone. It was a ring with a dark green stone which had little red lines in it.

'It belonged to Douglas's mother,' Cosette said. I knew about Douglas's mother and the way she had died, the same way my mother was going to die.

Possibly I wasn't as kind to her as she was to me, but I always loved her. When we are young we are often unkind.

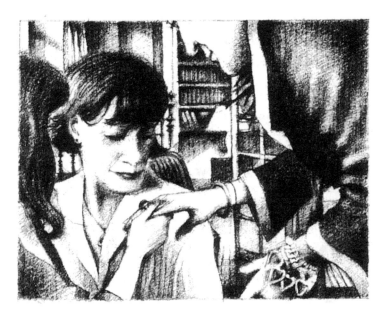

That is when I first saw the bloodstone. It was a ring with a dark green stone which had little red lines in it.

At least Cosette never knew. She did not ask for anything from the people she loved; she only wanted to be able to give herself to them and feel safe, without the fear that they would betray her.

Douglas had never betrayed her. He had loved her and made her safe. She only had to follow the way of life he had chosen: the neighbours, the visits, the dinners, the cleaner, the cook and the gardener, the money and endless free time. Of course, it had to end – everything does – although it seemed to me that nothing would ever change for Cosette.

One autumn morning Douglas died in his Rolls-Royce on the way to work. He was fifty-three and had almost certainly passed the age when his inheritance could appear in him. His death had nothing to do with his inherited disease. It was his heart. The doctor told Cosette it happened so fast he probably didn't know anything about it.

Chapter 3   Old Friends

I wasn't living at Cosette's house when Douglas died; I was twenty and at university. My mother was dying, but I rushed to Cosette as soon as I heard. When I saw her she was crying.

Since then I have learnt that family and neighbours are always ready with advice for a woman in Cosette's situation. She was forty-nine, but looked older. Her hair was grey and her face tired, and she had put on weight. They told her she should move to 'a little place by the sea', or a cottage in the countryside, or a 'nice flat' outside town. Cosette didn't refuse openly; she just smiled and shook her head. Later I understood that she was silent because she had a different plan.

One day I heard one of Cosette's neighbours suggest that she ought to marry again. I was shocked. Those were days when life seemed to belong to the young and beautiful. I couldn't imagine Cosette having a man friend, a lover; she was too old. But I remembered the neighbour's words a year later when Cosette, alone with me, said suddenly, 'You always hear of men chasing after women. I'd like to be a woman who chases after men. Do you know what I'd like, Elizabeth? I'd like to be thirty again and steal everybody's husbands,' and she laughed a soft, hopeless laugh.

◆

I am sitting now at my writing-desk in this little house in Hammersmith where I live. I am looking at the things Cosette gave me, the typewriter (I wrote my first novel on it, at Archangel Place) and the books. The works of Henry James are there, and among them *The Wings of the Dove*. But this is not the same copy Bell picked up off my desk in the House of Stairs. She wanted to know the story, though Bell never read a book in her life.

On the desk in front of me I have a list of telephone numbers. I have found the numbers of some of the people I knew when I lived at Archangel Place. But why should any of them know where Bell is living now? They wouldn't want to know her; they may even hate her.

I phone Elsa. I have not seen or spoken to her for a month or two, but I know it doesn't matter: we will always be friends. The phone rings, but there is no answer. I try Esmond and Felicity. They used to live outside London and probably still have that house, but they also have a flat in London. The daughter answers the phone. Those children were three and six when I first went with Elsa to Thornham Hall; now they must be in their early twenties.

The girl tells me that her parents still live at Thornham and gives me their number. Then she says, what did I want to ask her parents about? Was it something about that woman who killed somebody – Christine something?

'Christabel Sanger,' I say, and then, 'but we called her Bell.'

'She phoned my mother a few weeks ago. She'd just come out of prison, I think. My mother could tell you more. Why don't you phone her?'

I thank her and say goodbye. So Bell is with us again. I feel a little sick. I won't phone Felicity yet. She'll want to know everything. She may ask me about Mark, or even about those last days at Archangel Place. I'll wait until tomorrow morning.

Chapter 4   Christabel

After my mother's death I went home to live with my father. But I spent my days with Elsa and at Cosette's house in Hampstead. Then I went for a week with Elsa to her relations in Essex.

Esmond came to meet us from the station and drove us out into the countryside. Thornham Hall was an enormous place, with fifteen bedrooms and a library and a morning-room, and surrounded by its own land. A cottage or two stood near it, and a farm. Esmond and Felicity lived there with Esmond's old mother. Felicity always needed entertainment, so she used to invite people to the house for parties, musical evenings, games and discussions. Sometimes, Elsa told me, the people from the cottage came up and joined them. They were friends of Felicity. Silas Sanger had in fact been an old boyfriend of Felicity. Now he lived with Christabel. He was a painter and a hard drinker, who sometimes behaved very strangely. Nobody knew anything about Christabel; she was a mystery.

I saw the painter's wife one afternoon as I sat looking out of a window with Felicity's daughter Miranda. Silas Sanger's cottage was very small, with an untidy garden. The curtains at the windows were torn and dirty. A tall girl appeared. With her soft, fair, untidy hair piled up on top of her head, her long neck and narrow waist, and her unusual clothes, she reminded me of a woman in a French painting. The girl began to hang some washing on the line, but she seemed bored and unhappy.

Two days after this there were guests at Thornham Hall. Felicity had arranged another of her little entertainments. She had invited the people from the cottage, but a note arrived from Bell, saying she didn't want to come. Felicity smiled at us.

'She's proud of always saying what she means.'

Felicity believed that Bell never told lies, even when she knew she might hurt people's feelings. Felicity believed this and we believed it too. But I was sorry; I had looked forward to meeting this mysterious woman.

Later that evening we were all sitting round the fire, playing a game, when the front door suddenly opened and Bell Sanger came in.

'Would somebody come, please? Silas has shot himself. He was drunk. He was playing one of his games. I think he's dead.'

Chapter 5   The House of Stairs

Felicity answers the phone. She doesn't sound surprised to hear me after all this time. She starts talking about her children, then I tell her I have spoken to Miranda.

'She told me you'd spoken to Bell Sanger. I thought you might give me Bell's address.'

Felicity is silent. Then her voice changes. 'Uh, my dear, I don't have it. I have a phone number. Six-two-four something.'

But she can't remember exactly. She promises to call back.

♦

When I got home from Thornham after the death of Silas Sanger, I told Cosette about it all. Felicity had explained to me about Silas's 'games'. He loved guns and used to play Russian roulette when he was drunk. When I saw him that night, he was lying in a pool of blood on the floor of his cottage. Bell was very calm. She said she had been upstairs and heard the shot. I believed her story then. Much later I found out that, a few hours before Silas died, his father had died, leaving him

£10,000. The money came to Bell and was just enough for her to live on.

I didn't know this when I was telling my story to Cosette. I waited for her to give her opinion. Instead of that she said, 'I have bought a house.'

I looked at her.

'It's in London. In Notting Hill. You'll like it. It's a big, tall house on five floors with 106 stairs. I call it the House of Stairs.'

'Notting Hill?' I said. It was a poor, dirty and dangerous part of London in those days.

'I won't be alone,' she said. 'People will come. Don't you think people will come?'

What people? Her Hampstead neighbours? Her rich friends?

'There are a lot of young people in that part of London,' said Cosette.

'But what will you do?'

'Live,' said Cosette, smiling. 'I mean I will just live there and – and wait and see.'

Chapter 6   A Break with the Past

Felicity phoned me this morning.

I asked her, 'Why did Bell phone you?'

'Oh, Elizabeth, I thought you knew. She wanted your number.'

I suddenly felt so happy I was ashamed of myself. Of course Felicity had not known my number. She gave me Bell's, but I don't want to call Bell yet.

♦

Cosette didn't plan to live alone in the House of Stairs; she was going to have one or two friends and relations with her. I finished university and travelled around Europe for a time. I had seen the House of Stairs twice and hadn't liked it. It was big, old, dirty and cold, with too many stairs and dangerous windows. On my third visit everything had changed. The rooms hadn't been repainted, but curtains had been put up, and there were new carpets and furniture. Cosette too was different. She had thrown out all those unattractive suits and dresses. When I came in and went up the stairs to find her sitting at her table, she was wearing bright yellow with red and white flowers. And that wasn't the only change. She had lost weight and her hair was a different colour.

'The hairdresser says it makes me look ten years younger.'

I didn't want to say I couldn't see it myself, so I just said she looked very nice, much better. This seemed to make her happy. We climbed up the stairs and she showed me 'my' room.

'You can come every weekend,' said Cosette.

She didn't talk about Douglas. It seemed as if she had not only changed her style of living but made a complete break with the past.

That evening people came, all of them young, students, hippies, I suppose. I don't know where they came from. Probably they came because it was free: the drink, the food, the cigarettes and a bed or a floor to sleep on. But they also came because of Cosette herself. You see, Cosette *was* looking for a lover, though I didn't know it then. To me she looked like these people's mother, but not an ordinary mother because she let them do whatever they wanted. She smiled at those young men with their long hair and beards, as they sat reading or playing the guitar. I didn't realize she was terribly lonely, so lonely that she would look for a lover among boys almost thirty years younger than her. It was only later, at Christmas, that she explained to me. That is when she talked to me about stealing other women's husbands.

'I want to be thirty again, Elizabeth. You know, I'd been

*She smiled at those young men with their long hair and beards,
as they sat reading or playing the guitar.*

married for eleven years when I was thirty. Girls married young in those days. But it's all changed now. I missed all this. Now I want to start living.'

By Easter she had succeeded, and a man called Ivor Sitwell was her lover.

Chapter 7   The Wings of the Dove

A little over a hundred years ago George Huntington described a disease which is now called 'Huntington's Chorea'. There is now a test to find out whether you have it, but it is complicated. They have to test your own blood and the blood of at least seven other members of your family. I haven't got seven living relations on my mother's side of the family. They have all died of Huntington's.

My grandmother had six children. She didn't know that her father had Huntington's. She didn't know that her own children might inherit it. My mother showed the first signs of the illness when she was thirty-six. Her hands and shoulders used to shake violently; in the end she lost all control over her body.

Perhaps twenty years ago there were enough of the family left to give blood for the test. But it is too late now. I only have to wait two or three more years and I will know.

♦

Without intending it, Ivor Sitwell brought Bell back into my life. At first it seemed impossible that any good could come from him. I remember the shock when I found him in the House of Stairs.

Ivor was a writer, Cosette told me. He was a thin, unhealthy-looking man, with a bony face and very long brown hair. Most young men had long hair then, but Ivor wasn't very young – he was about forty. I disliked him immediately. He seemed to be interested only in himself and was usually rude to Cosette. It was obvious to me that he was using her; he wanted her money. I felt lost, like a child who finds out that her mother has a lover.

But Ivor didn't stay for long. Cosette saw him one day lying in the park with a girl he had met at the house. She couldn't forgive him – he had betrayed her – and refused to let him in the house again.

But all this was in the future. Ivor Sitwell was still living with Cosette and sharing her bed and insulting her. Then one day he arranged that Cosette and I should meet a friend of his. This is where I saw Bell again, at this friend's house.

Ivor had told us that there was a young woman who had a room in the house. Cosette and I arrived late, but Ivor wasn't there. We waited with Ivor's friend. Then I heard the front door open and Ivor talking with somebody. The door to the room opened and he came in with Bell.

Ivor immediately began telling us how he had met Bell on the steps outside. I don't know if she recognized me or if Ivor had already told her about the visitors. She looked at me and said very calmly, 'Hallo, Lizzie,' as if we had last seen each other the day before.

She was all in black – like Milly Theale in *The Wings of the Dove*. Ivor tried to start a conversation with her, but she turned her back on him. Bell said to me, 'Come up and see where I live.'

So I left the room and went upstairs with Bell. She had lived there since she left Thornham, she told me. There was very little in her room except for the bed, a table and a chair.

'What do you do?' I asked. 'Do you work?'

'I don't work.' She looked pleased when she said this. 'I don't work at all. I'm *never* going to work.'

'Then you're rich?'

Her eyes opened wide. 'I'm not, I'm not rich. But I hate working. I've got just enough to live on without working, if I live in a place like this.'

She laughed and her face was beautiful. I was excited by her. But what did I want of her? Did I want a friend? Did I want somebody to talk to and be with? And what did she want? I know now, of course I know, but I didn't know then. She was young and beautiful and healthy and intelligent, but she chose to live in that dark little room in that dirty house, without a job or a future. And I discovered later that she didn't have a lover or even many friends.

That September Cosette and I went to Italy together. She had intended to go with Ivor, but by that time Ivor had gone.

In Florence, at the Uffizi, there is a painting by Bronzini of Lucrezia Panciatichi. This is the painting that Henry James describes in *The Wings of the Dove*. The woman in the painting looks like Milly Theale, James's heroine. She also looked a lot like Bell. I bought a copy of the picture while I was in Italy and hung it in my bedroom in the House of Stairs when I got back.

Chapter 8   Meeting Bell Again

I was standing in front of this picture in my room this afternoon when Bell phoned.

This picture has followed me everywhere since the House of Stairs was sold. Sometimes it has seemed to bring bad luck, so I have been afraid to have it on the wall. But three days ago I hung it here in my study. It is years since I have looked at it and there are things I never noticed before – for example, the fact that Lucrezia is wearing a single ring with a very dark stone in it, which may even be a bloodstone.

She only said 'Hallo', but I didn't doubt for a second that it was her. I was silent in shock.

'It's Bell.'

'I know,' I said. 'Oh, I know.' I sat down, suddenly feeling a great tiredness.

'Will you come and see me?' she said.

That is why I am here, sitting opposite her now. The room is very like the room in Ivor's friend's house where I was first alone with her. There is a bed, a table, a chair and a couple of suitcases. Bell tells me that they found this place for her when she came out of prison. They have also found a job for her in a shop.

She is very changed in appearance, though still thin and straight, with that head held high on her long neck. There are lines on her face. She wears black. I haven't touched her yet, I haven't shaken her hand or kissed her.

When I came to the door and she brought me up here, she remembered. 'Are you past the age, are you safe yet?'

It seemed the kindest thing.

'Nearly,' I said.

♦

When Cosette and I came back from Italy, Bell had moved away from Ivor's friend's house and disappeared. She had gone, without leaving a message for me. Perhaps she was with a man – or a woman – or perhaps she just couldn't pay for the room any more. She had never spoken of any friend or relation, or even of mother, father, brothers or sisters. I knew very little about her, except that she was very honest about her feelings and opinions, while she knew everything about me.

Cosette had given me a room near the top of the house, as a writing-room. I wrote my first three books there. That winter of 1969 I started to write my first novel, using Cosette's old typewriter.

Chapter 9   Mark

In the spring I went with a boyfriend to the theatre and afterwards to the theatre's café. It was months since I had seen Bell, but she was in the café that night. I saw her sitting at a table in the corner with two other girls and two men. One of these men was very much like her in appearance, darker but with the same sort of face. Before I reached the table and said hallo to her, he got up and went to the food bar.

'Is that your brother?' I said.

She turned to look at him for a moment. Then she nodded. 'Yes. Yes, it is. Good-looking, isn't he?'

'He's like you.'

'Perhaps you're right. Do you like him? Would you like to meet him?'

'I'm with somebody,' I said, 'and I have to go.' And then, 'Why don't you come round. I'd love to see you.'

That was the first time I saw Mark. Perhaps it was true that I liked him – he was very attractive. But my boyfriend was getting jealous and I soon forgot Mark. I naturally didn't know he was going to be so important in our lives. I only thought of Bell, hoping she would come.

A week later she came. There was a crowd of us in the living-room with Cosette. I remember Cosette was wearing the bloodstone, probably to match her new dark green dress. She still hadn't found the lover she wanted. Bell looked around at the other people in the room, the couple lying on the floor, the boy playing the guitar. Then she went up to Cosette, shook her hand and spoke to her. But she didn't waste any time with the others. She had come to see me.

'Can we go up to your room?'

I understood she meant the room I wrote in, not my bedroom. On the stairs – there were 106, remember, to the top, 95 to my writing-room – she said, 'They're all using her, aren't they? All getting something from her. Does she know?'

'I don't think that matters to her.'

'It would matter to me. I'd throw them out.'

'Cosette would never do that.'

Bell never read a book, but if there were books lying around she used to pick them up and look at them. We lit cigarettes and she walked about the room, looking at everything. She was very surprised that I was writing a novel.

It was raining when the time came for her to go. She didn't want to tell me her address and said she didn't have a phone.

'I could get a taxi,' she said, 'but I haven't got enough money. And if Cosette knows, she'll pay for it. I don't want that.'

Nobody else among Cosette's visitors thought like that. Bell was strangely pure, I thought. She just wanted to borrow a raincoat, so we went downstairs to my bedroom. I opened the door, forgetting that the picture of Lucrezia was hanging on the opposite wall. The light came on and Bell looked straight at the picture. She stood silent in front of it while I looked for the coat. Then, 'That's me,' she said.

I was embarrassed. 'It was painted about 400 years before you were born.'

'It's still me. Where did you get it? Did you put it there because it looks like me?'

'Yes,' I said.

I held out my black raincoat and she put it on. Then Bell took my face in her hands and kissed my mouth. I was shaking, but I said, very lightly, 'You mustn't get wet.'

Until they came and took her away, I never lost Bell again after that. She often came to see me at the House of Stairs. We used to talk a lot about other people, about the people who

I opened the door, forgetting that the picture of Lucrezia was hanging on the opposite wall.

lived in the house and those who passed through it. Bell was as interested in people as I was; that was one of the things I liked so very much about her. She really wanted to get inside people's heads and know them. I learnt a lot from Bell.

One day we were talking about Ivor Sitwell.

'Cosette is lucky he's gone,' she said. 'Do you think she'd like somebody else?'

'She'd like somebody she could love and who would love her. Wouldn't we all?'

Bell gave me a strange look; she didn't reply. Why did Cosette marry Douglas, I wondered aloud.

'Women get married to have somebody who will keep them,' Bell said quite seriously. 'They get married to be safe.'

I asked her about Silas. Why had she married Silas?

She was at art school, she told me, and she met Silas there. He was her teacher. Then he lost his job.

'So you didn't marry to have somebody who would keep you,' I said.

'Yes, I did. Partly. I knew he had an old dad who was ill and who'd leave him something. In fact, I thought it was more than it was. But I wasn't completely wrong, was I? I did get it – and it keeps me – just.'

We said good-night soon after that and I went down to my own room. Bell was going to stay the night in the room at the top. I was pleased that at last I had found out something about Bell's past. I didn't realize – like everybody, I believed Bell was always honest – that most of her story was a lie.

Chapter 10   The Living Lucrezia

In Venezuela there is a village where nearly everybody has Huntington's Chorea. I read this in today's paper. Huntington's has become a fashionable disease. I will be forty next week and Bell was right: I am probably safe now. I have been to meet Bell this morning after her first day at the shop. She was surprised to see me, but very pleased.

She has come home with me. I didn't ask her; somehow she decided. I am sitting opposite her now with a glass in my hand. We have been talking for almost two hours, but she hasn't spoken about Mark or Cosette.

♦

In the spring Cosette was ill. In fact she wasn't really ill at all, but she was frightened and she frightened me. Because I loved her so much I didn't want to lose her. I was sure that she was dying of cancer and I told Bell about my fears.

'When will you know what's wrong with her?'

'In about a week,' I said.

I didn't see Bell for some time after that conversation. She had never wanted to tell me where she was living, but by this time I had found out that she went to her mother's flat in Harlesden. When she left Ivor's friend's house, she said, she hadn't had anywhere to go. And her mother wasn't well, she needed somebody with her.

Cosette went into hospital and they found it was nothing serious. When I next saw Bell it seemed as if she had forgotten about it, so I never talked to her about it again.

Cosette wanted Bell to come and live at the House of Stairs.

'Bell has to live with her mother,' I said.

'I'm sure there's room for your mother too.'

Bell laughed. 'I'll think about it, Cosette.'

21

But Cosette made us go up to the top, into the room above my writing-room. She apologized for the room, the 106 stairs, the low ceiling and dangerous window.

'I'll have something done to make it safe,' Cosette said.

The window was frightening when you stood close to it. It came right down to the floor and, when it was open, it was like a doorway without a door. You looked down into the garden almost fourteen metres below.

Nothing was done about the window, though. And although she had to look after her mother, Bell stayed and slept up there that night. The next day she told me she had met a friend of her mother's who might be able to come and share her mother's house.

A week later we were looking through Cosette's clothes. Cosette was going to the theatre and wanted to find something suitable to wear. We found a long red dress that reminded me of the dress that Lucrezia Panciatichi is wearing in Bronzini's painting.

'Have it,' said Cosette. 'I'm never going to wear it again.'

Bell was in her usual dusty black. We were alone in the house, Bell, Cosette and I.

'I want you to put the dress on,' I said to Bell.

At first she refused. She said it was silly, her hair was wrong and she hadn't any jewellery. But, as she stood there looking at the picture, she started to like the idea. While she was changing, I went down to Cosette's room. We were talking about the book I had just finished when the door opened and Bell came in. Or Lucrezia Panciatichi came in – or Milly Theale. She had done her hair to look like the picture. Instead of smiling at our delight, she stood seriously, then sat in a chair and became the picture completely.

Cosette found the bloodstone and put it on her finger. Bell was calm, not laughing, not even smiling. Afterwards Bell and I

Cosette apologized for the room, the 106 stairs, the low ceiling and dangerous window.

went up to sleep. The stairs were dark. Bell took my hand in hers and led me. In my room the light was soft, coming from the small bed-lamp. The painted Lucrezia looked down at the living Lucrezia. Bell pushed the door closed with her toe. Oh, the house was so silent! We kissed, and entered each other's arms.

Chapter 11   In Love

Today is Sunday. I never write on Sundays and Bell doesn't have to go to work in the shop. The job makes her very tired. She goes to sleep as soon as she comes home. By 'home' I mean my house. She has returned here every day.

When she came down this morning, smoking her first cigarette of the day, she seemed less ghostly, younger and fresher looking. She even smiled. As we sat opposite each other later on, we knew that we had to talk. She began.

'Has Felicity ever told you she thought I might be responsible for Silas's death?'

I nodded.

'Nobody said anything about it at my trial, did they? All that about my childhood came out, all that. And I'd forgotten it. I'd forgotten about Susan. But that was why I went to prison for so long. They found out about Susan, but they never found out about Silas.' She took another cigarette and lit it. 'I killed him,' she said. 'Well, isn't it obvious?'

And she told me how she had fixed Silas's gun so that the game of Russian roulette would kill him.

'If it's true that you did it, why did you do it?'

'I was so sick of him, so bored. He married me to get a servant. God, I hated him.'

'Why didn't you divorce him?'

She looked at me strangely. 'His old father was dying,

wasn't he? And he was rich. Well, Silas said he was. So when the telegram came saying his father was dead, I didn't show it to him. I kept it to myself and fixed his gun.' Another cigarette. 'Have you still got that picture?'

'What picture, Bell?' Though I knew, of course I knew.

'The one of the girl in the red dress that somebody wrote a book about?'

'It's in my writing-room.' I said.

'I haven't been in there yet,' she said, and then, 'Can we go out? I'd like to go down to the river and go to a pub. Could we find a pub and eat there?'

♦

I have never wanted any other woman before or since. On the other hand I never felt it was a shocking thing. It is impossible for me to say how I felt then except that I was in love.

Bell moved into the top room in the House of Stairs. I don't know if Cosette knew about us, but I think she didn't; she probably saw us only as 'best friends'.

Bell was in my writing-room one day in early autumn as I was just finishing work. She picked up a book off my desk and asked, 'Is this the one about the girl that looks like me?'

'No, that's *The Wings of the Dove.*' I found my copy of James's novel and gave it to her.

'What's it about?' she asked.

So, sitting there on the floor with Bell next to me, I told her the story of *The Wings of the Dove*. That was all, nothing more. But Milly Theale stayed in her memory. I suppose the painting made her remember it.

She said slowly, wonderingly. 'What a clever idea!'

'James was clever. There has never been a cleverer novelist.'

Chapter 12   Waiting for a Man

The first time Mark came to Archangel Place there were about eight people living in the House of Stairs. Bell was there of course. In the autumn of 1972 she had gone back to her mother in Harlesden for a time. I know now that Bell didn't have a mother in Harlesden, that her parents were living in a small town by the sea, trying to forget that they were parents. But I didn't know it then. I believed Bell when she said she had to go 'home' for a time.

I am sure that Bell's feelings for me were once as real as mine for her, but they had now begun to weaken. Her thoughts were somewhere else. I had finished my second book and I was busy. Then she went back to her mother's. There was an awful evening when we sat together in the garden, Cosette and I. Each of us was feeling lonely. I remember Cosette said, 'Why does nobody come any more?'

I put my arms around her. I knew she was waiting for a man to come, a lover, a husband. Women are usually shy about saying they need a man. Not Cosette. She said it to everybody. Her life was sad. The man hadn't come.

But two days later he came. Bell brought him. She had been absent for two or three weeks, then reappeared in the House of Stairs as if she had never been away.

'My brother's coming this evening,' she said. 'Is that all right?'

Mark – how can I describe him? He was simply the best-looking man I have ever known and one of the nicest. Or at least I thought so for a long time. He was always kind, warm and gentle. He was older than Bell, with brown skin and hair.

Cosette wasn't looking very good that evening. Her hair was untidy and she had put on weight again. Any of the other young women in the room had a better chance than her. When Mark walked in you could see all their eyes on him. It was the way he

Mark – how can I describe him? He was simply the best-looking man I have ever known.

moved, as well as his appearance. He walked like a dancer. It was sad to see that Cosette had already stopped hoping. She put out her hand to him with a half-smile.

Mark didn't talk about himself. Bell told me he was an actor and worked in radio, and that he was single. Mark was a listener and for a time we knew only that he was pleasant and interesting. Later, at dinner, when Cosette made a joke, he laughed and I saw Cosette redden. I was afraid for her, I was already afraid.

Cosette fell in love with him that evening. I saw the way she looked at him and I watched fearfully. It would pass, I thought, it *must* pass; a week later he would be forgotten. But Cosette wasn't going to let that happen. She wasn't going to let him get away. She wanted to fix a date for his next visit. She knew that Bell's birthday, her thirtieth, was coming soon, so she invited Mark to Bell's birthday party. Her face was shining. It was impossible not to see her happiness.

Later that night, lying in bed next to Bell, I said to her, 'Cosette is going to fall in love with Mark.'

'She's in love with him already.'

'I'd like to stop it somehow.'

'Why? Because you're afraid he'll make her unhappy? But he'll be different. He won't be like that Ivor person. Mark will be kind to her, you'll see.'

♦

This morning we went shopping together, Bell and I. She has lost the job in the shop and is staying with me. She doesn't say it, but I know she is going to stay here. Once this was my dream; now I don't want it at all. Bell is too much for me, her past is too much, the things she has done. It has made me nervous, all of it. It is causing the kind of worry that doctors have always warned me about. Sometimes my hand shakes.

My fortieth birthday has passed and gone. Bell and I went out to dinner. Afterwards I tried to get her to talk about Mark and Cosette, but she talked about Silas.

'Do you want to know how I really met Silas? It was in the children's home. The home was a big house, with big children mixed up with little children. It was one of those modern ideas they wanted to try out. A disaster, actually. Give me my cigarettes, will you?

'They put me in there when I was sixteen, that was in 1958. But they weren't modern enough to send me to school. I went out to work. I wanted to get away. Silas came to the home sometimes. A relation of his had a child there. Felicity was his girlfriend then. So I got him away from her and got married to him. That way I got out.'

'Is that true, Bell?'

'Of course it is.'

I couldn't control the painful nervous movements in my neck and shoulders. 'Where was Mark then?' I said. 'What was Mark doing?'

She jumped up and ran out of the room.

♦

Mark came to the party Cosette gave for Bell's birthday. At that party Cosette gave Bell the bloodstone ring. Mark didn't stay long; he went home a little after midnight. Cosette wanted him to come back the following evening to dinner, but Mark refused politely.

I was angry with him; it was unkind. Or was he trying to make himself more interesting, difficult to get? Cosette watched him leave. Then we were alone.

'I'd give everything I've got if I could be young again,' Cosette said.

Chapter 13   Just Friends

I thought we would never see Mark again, and I was surprised when about a week later he rang to ask Cosette out to dinner. Just the two of them. I thought Cosette would be excited, but she seemed quite calm. I think she had stopped hoping for anything in that direction.

'I'm trying to prepare myself so that when the people in the restaurant think I'm his mother I can just smile,' she said to me.

I didn't see her go or return. Next morning Mark was there in the living-room with Cosette.

'He probably stayed the night,' Bell said.

But we found out from the others in the house that he hadn't.

Mark was just a friend. He took Cosette out to meals. But he didn't often come with us when Cosette was paying. He wasn't using her.

♦

Bell has told me about Silas, but she still refuses to talk about Mark or Cosette. She has talked about herself and me.

'There weren't any women before you,' she said. 'There haven't been any since.'

'Then why...?'

She said simply, 'Because you wanted to. That night when I put the dress on, I thought you'd like it.'

'Didn't *you*?'

'Oh, sure. I loved it. But it was never the real thing, was it?'

I couldn't look at her. There was one question I had to ask.

'Were you ever in love with me?'

She obviously didn't want to hurt me. 'I don't know. I liked you a lot. I liked the feeling of doing something that might shock people.'

♦

As Mark came to the house more often and he and Cosette went out more together, Bell and I became more distant from one another. I didn't know then that she didn't love me, had never loved me. We talked less too. Cosette had bought a television and Bell spent a lot of time watching it. I thought perhaps she didn't like the fact that Mark was spending so much time with Cosette. Had Cosette separated her from her brother? Perhaps also Cosette had taken the place of a sister in Mark's life. Certainly there wasn't any sign that she and Mark were more than friends to each other. Mark had never become like Ivor Sitwell. He never stayed the night.

Once he spoke of her to me. We were having dinner in a

restaurant and Cosette had gone to pay the bill. Mark turned to me.

'I've never known anybody like her,' he said. 'She is the most wonderful person; she has everything.'

Cosette didn't usually talk about herself and her feelings, but one evening she started to talk to me.

'I'm so much in love with him I think it will kill me.'

'Mark?' I said stupidly.

'I didn't know it could be like this. It was never like this before. No, not with Douglas, never, never. Don't look at me like that, Lizzie.'

'I'm sorry,' I said.

'I think of him day and night. When he's not with me I'm thinking of him and talking to him. I have these long conversations with him in my head.'

I said carefully, 'Perhaps love is not so good if it isn't returned – I mean if the other person doesn't feel the same.'

Cosette's reply shook me. She almost shouted, 'Who says he doesn't feel the same?' She looked at me, her hands stretched out to me.

'I don't want you to be unhappy,' I said quietly. I couldn't think of anything else to say, so I went over to her and held her in my arms.

Chapter 14 In the Will

We have had a visitor, Bell and I. It is two weeks since Bell came to stay. Then yesterday my father came. Twice a year he comes to London to see a doctor. He is seventy-three now and his heart is weak. Afterwards he comes back here to stay the night.

It may seem strange that he doesn't know anything about Bell and me, but I didn't tell him about her at the time and I didn't have to appear at her trial. So he doesn't know that Bell is the Christabel Sanger who appeared in every newspaper and on television for a couple of days all those years ago.

My father has changed. He has succeeded in forgetting my mother's death. And he talks of the distant future, *my* distant future, as if I was safe already. His little house and his money (he has tried to save a few pounds) are all for me, he says.

'It's all in my will.'

'It's much too soon to think of that,' I said.

'It's easy to say that at your age. But it can happen at any time, you know.'

Bell was watching him with a strange look on her face. I suppose she was surprised that he refused to recognize the fact that I was still in danger. Or perhaps he reminded her of the evening when she had asked me about Cosette's will. I didn't ask. I'm not yet ready to start a discussion with her about Mark and Cosette.

♦

I was at the typewriter in the working-room in the House of Stairs, listening to Bell as she moved about in the room above me. I heard a noise on the 104th stair. She came in and picked up a book.

'I suppose,' she said suddenly, 'Cosette will leave everything to you.'

'*What?*'

'In her will, I mean. When she dies this house and all her money will go to you.'

'But she's not going to die.'

Bell stood with her back to the window. 'She's got cancer, hasn't she?'

'What gave you that idea?'

She didn't say anything at first. I was suddenly afraid. Did she know something that I didn't?

'I thought they found cancer when she went into hospital for those tests.'

'They didn't find anything. She was perfectly clear. She'll probably live for thirty years. She'll live longer than I will.'

Bell seemed to think deeply and enormously. 'I see,' she said slowly, and again, 'I see.'

I was angry. I thought she was selfishly afraid of losing her place in the House of Stairs. She wanted to be sure that her 'friend' would still be able to keep her after Cosette died. She didn't seem to have any feelings for Cosette at all. I felt she was using me. Was it possible that she had got close to me simply because she thought I was going to inherit a lot of money from a rich woman?

That autumn Cosette became much richer than before. Douglas had left her a piece of land just outside London. A new road was planned and the land was suddenly very valuable. Cosette wasn't the sort of person who could keep quiet about things like this. She told the news to all her visitors.

'Hundreds of thousands of pounds,' she said.

Bell was there to hear it that evening, and Mark too, of course. I looked at her. I thought she might look at me, weighing the advantages of staying friends with me. But she wasn't looking in my direction. She was looking at Cosette. How could anybody imagine that Cosette was ill with cancer, I wondered? She seemed so obviously happy and her happiness made her beautiful. She had lost weight and her skin looked healthier, her hair shone. She had changed her style of dress too and had become really attractive.

Bell stood up and said that she was going to Thornham for the Christmas holiday again. She was going the next day. Did she know then that it was going to be the last time?

It was late and Cosette asked Mark to stay the night. This time he said he would. I was shocked. I thought he meant with her, in her bed, and I didn't want that; but I was wrong. When Cosette had gone upstairs, Mark said to me, 'There's a room I can sleep in at the top, isn't there?'

I nodded. 'Next to Bell. The door on the right. The one on the left is Bell's.'

I lay in bed thinking about their future, Mark and Cosette. One day, of course, he would marry and she would be terribly hurt. But the pain would pass and they would probably still be friends.

Soon after that Mark lost his job. I had always felt he was different from the rest of the crowd who lived off Cosette and her money; he had been the only one with a job. But as the weeks went by and still he hadn't found any work, I started watching him. When was he going to start borrowing money from her, I wondered?

Chapter 15   Changes

Today I asked Bell about that last Christmas at Thornham.

'Just the same,' she said. 'It was always the same. I don't know why I went.'

'Don't you?'

She looked at me as if she refused to talk about it.

'You went so that you wouldn't see those two together,' I said, 'so that you wouldn't be there when *it* happened.'

She gave an unpleasant laugh. 'Do you mean Mark and Cosette? Do you mean I didn't want to be there the first time he slept with her? Do you think it mattered to me? I only wanted him to be quick about it. God, he was so slow. In fact I thought he'd do it faster if I wasn't there.'

'I want to know something. Did you,' I said carefully, 'plan to kill Cosette from the beginning?'

'I had the idea she was going to die naturally.'

'But when you knew she didn't have cancer, were you planning it then?'

Her reply was so open, a loud laugh. 'Planning it? You know I don't plan. I don't plan to kill somebody. I do that' – she spoke quite proudly – 'with a quick decision. Even Silas – I thought about it often enough, but I was only planning for about five minutes. It's only when things get impossible or I – I want something very very much.'

She got up and went upstairs to lie down.

♦

That last Christmas the house was full. Full of loving couples, it seemed. Cosette's lodgers all had their boyfriend or girlfriend staying with them. You used to find them lying on sofas or sitting in quiet conversation on the stairs or kissing in dark corners.

And, of course, there were Mark and Cosette. It was obvious that they were in love, he with her and she with him. But they were different from the other couples. Occasionally their hands touched, but nothing more. Perhaps it was their age. *Their* age? Mark was not much older than me. But while Cosette seemed younger than ever before, Mark had grown older than his real age, so they were somehow more equal. But they weren't yet lovers in the modern meaning of the word.

Everything changed a few evenings after Christmas. We were sitting lazily, listening to music and drinking Cosette's wine, when Mark and Cosette came in. They joined us, Mark sitting on the arm of Cosette's chair. He bent and kissed her lips. It was the first time I had ever seen them kiss. Cosette smiled, spoke his name only, 'Mark . . .'

He gave her his hand. 'Shall we go?' he said.

It was obvious that they were in love, he with her and she with him.

I thought he meant he was going home. But we all heard them climbing the stairs together. It was like a wedding night. Her door shut and nobody came down.

When I told Bell, she smiled. She was pleased and took me in her arms. It was the first time for months and the last time ever.

Mark was now living in the House of Stairs. In a way he had started to control the house. Slowly he succeeded in driving most of the lodgers out. Sometimes I saw him looking at Bell as she lay on Cosette's sofa, smoking and watching television. Perhaps she would be the next to go. I was very afraid of that.

Soon after that he asked me to have dinner with him. Cosette was going to be away and he said he wanted to talk to me. We met in the restaurant.

'What did you want to say to me, Mark?'

'Several things, really.'

I was fearful. 'Mark, what is it?' I asked.

And then he said it. It gave me a greater shock than if he had told me he was leaving Cosette and the House of Stairs.

'I suppose you must realize I'm terribly in love with Cosette.'

I just looked at him. I didn't say anything.

'It wasn't like that at first,' he said. 'Of course, I liked her. But then – well, I fell in love.' He laughed a little. 'I couldn't believe it at first. It seemed so – unlikely. You look surprised.'

As I listened I realized he meant it. It was true, there wasn't any doubt about that. And I felt enormously happy – happy for Cosette, that she was safe.

'But I'm not going to get married,' he went on. 'Cosette is very rich and it wouldn't be the right thing. Do you understand?'

I almost laughed. 'Some people would think you married her for her money,' I said.

'Yes.'

He then told me that Cosette and he didn't want to continue

living in the House of Stairs. They were going to buy a smaller place somewhere so that they could be by themselves.

'Bell will be happy for you,' I said.

His face was suddenly darker. 'Please don't say anything to Bell about this yet.' He looked young and afraid and strangely unhappy. 'Of course, we'll tell Bell in time. But not yet. In fact Cosette feels she'll have to do something for Bell. She's thinking of buying her a flat.'

We talked of other things after that, but I was trying to understand: why would Cosette want to buy a flat for Bell? Because Bell was going to lose her room in the House of Stairs? Had Mark asked her to do it?

'Are you really going to buy Bell a flat?' I asked Cosette the next day.

'Well,' she said, 'Mark seems to think she won't be happy when we sell this house. He thinks she wouldn't feel so bad if we helped her a little.'

'Why would she feel bad?'

'She'll lose her home, won't she? I can understand it, although my dream now is to live alone with Mark in a little house somewhere. Do you think I'm completely mad? I love him so much. Oh, Elizabeth, I'm so lucky, I can't believe anybody can be so happy.'

I didn't tell Bell. In fact I never saw her; she stayed in her room and didn't want to see anybody. The House of Stairs had become a quiet place. Then Elsa came to stay.

Elsa had always been my best friend and is so still. She had divorced her first husband and needed a place to stay for a month or so. Mark wasn't very pleased, but I could see he was thinking that all this sort of thing would end soon. Bell didn't seem to see it, though. She was waiting for something to happen. She watched Mark, but he didn't even look at her any longer.

Bell was letting me know that she didn't want to talk to me. It was as if I had been useful for a time but now she didn't need me. If I spoke to her, she answered — that was all. When we all sat together in Cosette's living-room, she was never with us.

One day she walked in while I was there with Elsa and Mark and Cosette, drinking coffee.

'I'd like to speak to you,' she said to Mark. 'Upstairs.'

I thought he would say that she needn't be afraid to speak in front of Cosette, but he didn't. He got up and left the room with her.

'It's about having a key to her room,' Cosette said.

Some days later Elsa said to me, 'Mark is a weak sort of person, isn't he?'

'Why do you say that?'

'Well, he's afraid of Bell. Somebody's coming to look at this house tomorrow — somebody interested in buying it, I think — and he doesn't want her to know. He asked me to take her out somewhere so that she's not in when this man comes.'

Bell was beginning to guess. At least she knew something had gone wrong. She knew he was hiding something from her. That was why she wanted to talk to him privately. I'm sure he wasn't brave enough to tell her. He probably said that things were going well, that she must be patient.

Chapter 16   We Learn the Truth

This morning we were in Bell's room at her old address. We packed Bell's things into a suitcase. She is moving into my house. I don't look forward to it very much.

Among the things we packed into the suitcase I found the bloodstone. I looked at it closely for the first time. It has passed down in our family, probably from one diseased member to

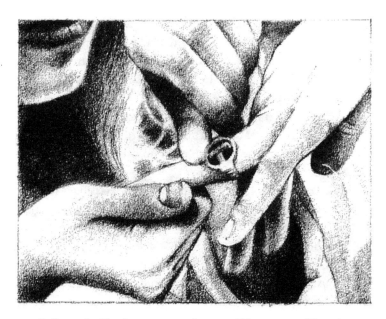

Bell put the bloodstone on my finger as if it was a wedding ring.

another, until it finally came to Douglas's mother, my mother's aunt.

'You can have it,' Bell said.

Her words surprised me. She put the bloodstone on my finger as if it was a wedding ring, and laughed. I don't understand her, I don't know what she wants. For example, she seems to be able to live with so little; we filled one suitcase and the room was empty. I said something about this to her.

'If I can't have the things I want,' Bell said, 'I prefer to have nothing.'

We went downstairs and into the street, looking for a taxi. But there weren't any taxis, so we began to walk. Then Bell remembered the friend who lived near there.

'We could go and see Elsa,' she said.

Until now she has never wanted to see anybody from the past. Elsa probably knew that Bell was living with me. She invited us to stay and have lunch with her.

♦

Elsa refused to take Bell out so that she wouldn't see the man who was coming to look at the house. Elsa is truly honest and open. And it wasn't necessary; the man didn't want to see everything and didn't go up as far as Bell's room.

That night we all went out to dinner at a restaurant. Bell had agreed to come, to my surprise. But none of us got as far as having dinner. We all had drinks, I remember that. Cosette was wearing a new dress and was looking very nice, her face peaceful and happy. Somebody was telling a joke when a woman came up behind Mark and touched him on the shoulder. She was about forty, dark and attractive. He looked round, immediately pushed back his chair and got up. She kissed him on the cheek.

Mark didn't turn white; his face was empty. He said, 'Hallo, Sheila,' then said our names, 'Cosette, Elsa, Elizabeth . . .' but she stopped him with 'Of course I know Bell!'

She was looking at Bell and smiling. Bell was holding her glass in both hands and looking silently in front of her. By this time it was clear that something was wrong. At least it was clear to everybody at our table but not to the woman called Sheila.

'I'm Sheila Henryson. I'm Mark's sister-in-law,' she said.

She turned and called a man over to our table. He didn't look much like Mark, but, when you knew, you could see he was Mark's brother. That meant he must be Bell's brother too, didn't it?

Sheila Henryson didn't seem to notice the looks on our faces. Her husband came up and said something to Mark. Cosette was the first of us to speak. She said to Mark's brother. 'Then Bell is your sister?'

41

*A woman came up behind Mark and touched him on the shoulder.
She was about forty, dark and attractive.*

'No,' he said. 'What makes you think that?'

I heard Bell make a sound. Cosette didn't turn white either, but she seemed to get suddenly older. She put out a hand as if to touch Mark. Mark's brother gave a nervous laugh.

'Have I said something wrong?'

A waiter arrived with some food, but Cosette put her hand over her mouth, got up and walked out of the restaurant. Everybody began talking at once.

The brother said to Mark, 'But what did I *do*?'

Mark didn't answer; he went after Cosette. The others left and I followed Elsa and Bell. Elsa asked the question I hadn't been able to ask: 'Why did you say he was your brother?'

Bell gave a look of hopelessness. She pointed at me. 'It was her idea. She said, is he your brother? I thought it would work better. And it *was* working until that stupid woman spoiled everything.'

'What do you mean, work better?' I said.

She didn't answer. 'He's my lover,' she said.

I think I gave a cry. 'Since when?' I was as interested in this as Elsa.

'Years.'

We were walking along the street, a street of restaurants, clubs and small shops. That sort of shock gives you a pain. I felt as if I had run too fast. I wanted to sit down. Elsa stood and looked at me, then she spoke to Bell. 'Why don't you just go?'

Bell walked away and disappeared round a corner. Elsa and I stayed there some time. I was thinking: what did this mean to me, the fact that Mark was Bell's lover, and what would it mean to Cosette? Then we got a taxi and went home in it.

The house appeared to be empty. Cosette's car wasn't there. That made me feel better; perhaps Mark and Cosette had gone out somewhere in it together.

Elsa and I waited. I could only lie in a chair and look at the ceiling and think and think and feel awful.

'I don't think we'll see Bell again,' I said. 'She'll go to her mother.'

Elsa said, 'She told me she hasn't had any parents since she was twelve.'

'What happened when she was twelve? Did she say her parents were killed in an accident or something?'

'She told me only that she lost her parents. She went into some sort of home.'

'A children's home, do you mean?'

Elsa gave me a strange look. 'I don't think it was a children's home, not then, that came later. I don't know what it was.'

As she was speaking we heard the front door open and close downstairs. Somebody came up the stairs and passed the door. It must be Bell. We heard her go on up, walking heavily. We each held our breath. Even from down there you could hear the noise of the 104th stair. Her bedroom door closed.

Elsa smiled. 'She hasn't got a mother.'

We opened the windows. Cosette's car was now there. We saw Mark and Cosette get out. They stood looking at each other and then, there in the street, they went into each other's arms and kissed.

♦

Elsa behaves towards Bell as if she doesn't remember that evening all those years ago. After lunch, while we were having coffee, I watched Bell. She looks much better than the first day I met her again. She is getting younger. I could see Elsa looking at us and comparing. We had talked for two hours about unimportant things, and I still hadn't asked Elsa the question I always ask when we meet. Then Bell got up and went to the bathroom.

Quickly I asked my question. Elsa seemed to understand.

'Very well, I think. We spoke on the phone a couple of weeks ago.'

'I'm glad,' I said. 'I'm always glad. I don't suppose' – I never know how to ask this – 'anything is ever said about me?'

'Nothing, Lizzie, I'm sorry.'

I nodded a little. I could hear Bell coming back. I didn't want her to hear any secrets she shouldn't know.

Chapter 17   Losing Cosette

The phone was ringing when we came into my house. That was three days ago, but it seems a lifetime. My father was very ill in hospital. When Bell heard that I was leaving immediately to be with him, she said, 'Is he going to die?'

'I suppose so.'

'I'll be all alone here,' she said.

At the moment I am staying in my father's house. I spend most of my time at the hospital. I suppose it is natural to feel this way when your father is dying, but I have never known such a deep unhappiness and tiredness. I sleep a lot by my father's bedside and in front of the television in his house. But at night I lie awake with my head full of memories.

◆

That night fourteen years ago I fell asleep quickly. When I woke up I realized that, although things might end well for Cosette, they wouldn't for me. She still had Mark, but I had lost Bell. He had been Bell's lover. When, I asked myself, when was the last time? And suddenly I knew when it was. It was the night when Cosette asked Mark to stay and I had led him up to the top of the house, to the room next to Bell's.

That other night, after the restaurant, he had told Cosette

45

I could see that Cosette had cried a lot and I put out my hand to touch her on the arm.

everything. He had to, there wasn't any other possibility. He explained Bell's plan and his own part in it. And Cosette forgave him. Why wouldn't she? It isn't hard to forgive somebody who says you have saved him with your love. But somebody had to be guilty; Mark had to put the blame on somebody else.

The next day, in the early afternoon, I met Cosette on the stairs. Bell had been up in her room all day. I could see that Cosette had cried a lot and I put out my hand to touch her arm.

'Are you all right, Cosette?'

She stood there and looked at me. She pulled my hand off her arm.

'What is it, Cosette? What's the matter?'

She said, 'You brought that woman here.'

46

'Bell?' I was already cold with fear. 'But I didn't know.'

'It was your idea that Mark should pretend he was her brother.' I shook my head, but she went on. 'You gave her some book to read.'

'Bell? She's never read a book in her life.'

Cosette said quietly, 'She didn't need to read it. You told her the story. You gave her the whole wonderful idea. I suppose you made her see the similarity between the story and things here.'

It was too much for me to understand at once. Mark called from the bedroom and Cosette ran to him, shutting the door loudly behind her. I had had a shock. This was all completely wrong, but I was sure I could explain, I could make things right.

I sat in the kitchen and thought. Obviously Mark had told Cosette about *The Wings of the Dove*. Cosette thought I had given Bell the idea of doing what the lovers do in the novel. I remembered sitting with Bell that day and telling her the story.

'This man and girl want to get married, but they haven't any money. There's a young girl called Milly Theale who's very ill and enormously rich. The other girl suggests to her lover that he should marry Milly Theale. Then when Milly dies she'll leave him all her money and he and she can marry and enjoy it.'

Bell had thought Cosette had cancer. Mark would marry her, she would die and he would inherit her money; then he and Bell would live on it and enjoy it. But how had the plan changed when Bell found out that Cosette didn't have cancer? Had she intended to kill Cosette? I didn't think this then. These ideas came to me much later, when the facts about her sister Susan were known and Silas's death came into question.

Cosette and Mark went out together at about three-thirty. Later I found out that they had gone to make arrangements to get married. He was so weak, Mark; he wasn't even able to keep his first decision not to marry.

After a time I went out into the back garden and looked up at

Bell's window; it was wide open. I went up, hoping to talk to her, but she didn't open the door. I went down again and returned to the garden. Have I said that it was a very hot day? The heat lay over me like a heavy blanket.

As I sat there I understood something. I understood that Cosette was more important to me than Bell. If I lost Cosette I would have nothing. She was the one I had chosen to be my mother. I was frightened. A real mother would always forgive. But although I loved Cosette more than any mother, we weren't joined by blood. And although the bloodstone had passed down through Douglas's family, it hadn't passed from Cosette to me.

You see, my imagination was out of control. And still they didn't come back. It was the last time I sat in that grey garden, and almost my last day in the House of Stairs. Looking upwards, I saw Bell's head appear at her wide-open window.

The car returned. I heard it. I wanted to speak to Cosette. I wanted to hear her tell me it was all a mistake. But something made me wait. I waited, and the sun stood still. Minutes passed. I remember putting my head on my arms.

♦

Two days ago my father died. I have made all the necessary arrangements and came home yesterday. I enjoyed the peace and calm of my father's house without Bell, and wanted to delay my return. My father's house will be sold. It seems to be much more valuable than I thought. And the money my father has left – £20,000; I didn't imagine he had saved so much.

'Take it,' says Bell when I tell her about it. 'Unless you want to give some to me.' She laughs, so that I know she is joking. But, 'You could buy a bigger house for us now.'

It is an idea. Or I could buy her a flat and be free of her at last. But I won't do that. I feel as if I can't escape; I must live with Bell now. Of course, I am being silly, I am imagining things. She is very gentle with me today. She tells me that she has been to see Elsa again, that she walked to Archangel Place one day and looked at the house.

'Lizzie,' she said, 'Lizzie, what happened to Cosette?'

'I've been waiting for you to ask.'

'Is she dead?'

'No, she's not dead. She married an old friend of Douglas's, an old neighbour from Hampstead, and went back there to live.'

Chapter 18   Murder

I have shocked her and she has gone quite white.

'I thought she must be dead.'

'Why? She's only just seventy.'

Then I decide to tell her. I have never told anybody except Elsa.

'Cosette hasn't spoken to me since then, Bell. She has never forgiven me. She thinks I betrayed her, you see.'

'Why didn't you explain?'

'I didn't get the chance. After it happened, you see, that same evening, she didn't stay in the House of Stairs; her brother Leonard came and took her away. I phoned her, but she didn't want to speak to me. I was going to write, but what was I going to say? After your – trial, she went away somewhere, and when she came back I couldn't find her. Perhaps I didn't try very hard. I knew her, you see. I knew she couldn't forgive somebody who had betrayed her. Then Elsa told me she'd got married and I got married too and it was all too late.'

♦

When Mark and Cosette came home, they had made the arrangements for getting married. But there was one thing they

49

hadn't done yet: Mark must tell Bell. Or they must both tell Bell. Bell must be told.

Cosette never really understood. She thought Bell would be angry at losing her home and hoped to make peace by buying Bell a flat or something. Bell was going to hear that her lover was truly 'in love'. What would that mean to her? Cosette couldn't imagine. Mark, of course, knew better. He was frightened. He was probably afraid she would tell Cosette about their early plans without all the excuses and loving apologies.

You understand that I am guessing, don't you? You understand that I was not there, that he and Cosette were alone?

He went upstairs, up all 106 stairs, and knocked on her door. I don't know if she answered or if he just walked in. She was there in her room, lying by the wide-open window. He told Bell he had something to tell her.

After she had done it, but before the police came, she told Elsa and me the story. Isn't it strange that a person like Bell had never guessed Mark's true feelings?

'He said he was in love with her. The fool was standing by the open window. I knew he was going to marry her. That was part of the plan, that was great, fine. The house didn't matter. But he was in love with her? He was going away to live with her and drop me? He said, "I know about our plan, Bell. But I love her." And he turned his stupid face and looked at the sky as if the sun was smiling down at him.

'She came in then. She thought she ought to explain too. So I did it. I wanted to do it in front of her. You know what I did. I jumped up and ran at him and pushed him out. I wanted to do it, it was great – until I'd done it. Then I wanted to pull him back out of the air. Did you hear him scream, Lizzie, did you hear him scream?'

It is something I would like to forget, that awful cry as he fell. But it was nothing compared with the sound his body made when it hit the ground. I had gone inside the house and ran back outside. The broken thing lay spread on the ground. I turned towards the house and saw Elsa walking across the dining-room. Then, behind her, pushing her out of the way, Cosette ran into the garden and threw herself on to Mark's body. She lay on his body until at last they took her away. I saw she was covered with blood.

Some time later Bell came down and spoke to us, to Elsa and me. Somebody phoned the police. A police doctor lifted Cosette from Mark's body. Her face was terrible. They carried her to the sofa in the television room and the doctor gave her something to calm her. In the evening Leonard came for her.

I never saw her again.

I heard that she spoke at Bell's trial. I didn't. In English law murder means prison for life. Prisoners 'for life' usually come out after about ten years unless there is something else. There was something else in Bell's past: when she was twelve years old, the middle child of three, Bell had killed her baby sister.

She had spent her childhood in a special part of a women's prison. When she was sixteen she was taken to a children's home. Many people have told me they tried to kill their younger brother or sister. Most of these children fail because a parent comes in time. Bell succeeded — because her mother came too late.

But it taught her something: if you have killed once, you can kill again.

♦

Strangely, Bell has never forgiven Cosette. Cosette had said she would like to steal other women's men. And she had done it, she had stolen Bell's lover.

'You never told me how you met him,' I said.

'I met him that same evening you saw him, at the café. You

51

said, "Is that your brother?" It gave me a shock. My real brother, Alan, is so ugly and stupid, but Mark was beautiful, wasn't he? I thought, I'll say he's my brother and then perhaps I'll get to know him. Funny, wasn't it? I'd never seen him before.'

I knew she told lies for pure enjoyment. 'I don't believe it. He'd been at your table.'

'It wasn't my table. I was just there. I didn't know the others sitting there. When he came back – he was there alone too – I said to him that somebody had told me we looked like brother and sister; did he think we looked like each other? And that was it, Lizzie, that was the beginning of it. We had a drink and then we went back to his place together. He said he was glad he wasn't my brother. But you put the idea into my head. You've been wonderful at putting ideas into my head, Lizzie.'

So I have been responsible for it all. It all happened because of things I did and things I said, and Cosette was right to blame me. Perhaps it is the pain in my head that makes it all unreal. I haven't written anything for weeks. The headache never leaves me. There is something else too. I go to bed at night and fall asleep; but I wake up moments later with such a terrible fear inside me that my body jumps uncontrollably and my eyes, stretched wide open, look wildly into the empty darkness. It passes, in ten minutes or so it passes, and I go back to sleep. But what is it? And why does it come?

I told Bell. Put the light on, she said, drink something. Keep a glass of wine by your bed and drink that. I tried it, but I only succeeded in knocking the wineglass to the floor and the other things with it, my watch and the pills and the bloodstone ring. So I wear the ring all the time now, I never take it off.

We went to see a lawyer today. Bell suggested it, because I am really quite rich now and, if I die without a will, who will get it all, the two houses and my savings? There is nobody, they are all dead. I have left everything to Bell. The lawyer said he would send me the will so that I could sign it. It will be here by tomorrow.

I haven't told Bell about the other thing I have done. I have written to Cosette. I didn't want to do this, but when Bell told me about her first meeting with Mark I decided I would. I know Cosette will forgive me. I imagine her life now, the neighbours, the dinners, the visitors, the cleaner, the cook and the gardener. I dream of Cosette. I dream that she will come and save me. But save me from what? After fourteen years I have written to her and now, each time the phone rings, I start to shake.

Bell watches me. She watches me as if she is weighing her chances. She has been out looking at houses. I will probably do what she wants and buy one.

I think about the bloodstone. Sometimes I think it brings love, other times it seems to carry sickness and death through the family.

The phone is ringing. I jump up, wondering if I can in fact have a happy ending, wondering who will get to me first, Bell or Cosette. Or that third possibility that Bell hopes for . . .

I put out my hand to stop her getting up and I cross the room to answer the phone.

ACTIVITIES

Chapters 1–2

Before you read

1 Look at the Word List at the back of the book. Find words to match these descriptions.

    a your grandmother, for example.

    b a relative by marriage.

    c a person with long hair who was against violence.

    d something containing invented characters and events.

    e a thing that lawyers help you to write.

    f a place with a lot of young people.

    g to get something from a dead person.

    h to tell someone's secret to a third person, for example.

    i what people may do if their marriage doesn't work.

    j to agree silently.

2 Read the Introduction and answer these questions.

    a Where is the House of Stairs?

    b What is Bell's job?

    c Did Ruth Rendell have a happy family life?

    d What was her mother's problem?

    e In what way are Barbara Vine novels different from Ruth Rendell books?

3 The story is told in the first person (*'I'* not *'He/She'*). Look at the picture opposite page 1. Is the story-teller a man or a woman?

While you read

4 Tick (✓) the things that you learn in Chapters 1 and 2.

    a The story-teller hasn't seen Bell recently.   .....

    b Bell has been in prison.   .....

    c Cosette still lives in the House of Stairs.   .....

    d Bell shot her husband.   .....

    e The story-teller grew up happily with her parents.   .....

    f Cosette and the story-teller are relations by marriage.   .....

g Cosette is about forty years old now.   .....
h There is an inherited disease in the speaker's family.   .....
i Cosette's life with Douglas was comfortable but dull.   .....
j Douglas dies from his disease.   .....

After you read

5 Which of these people have the 'inheritance'?
   a Douglas
   b Cosette
   c the story-teller
   d the story-teller's mother
   e Douglas's mother
6 Which of these things will be important in the story, do you think?
   a Bell's hairstyle
   b the pain in the story-teller's legs
   c the back garden at Archangel Place
   d the bloodstone
7 Answer these questions.
   a Do we know why Bell has been in prison?
   b Do we know what Cosette blames the story-teller for?
   c How do we know that something happened at Archangel Place?
   d Why does the story-teller ask 'Why was I born at all?'

Chapters 3–5

Before you read

8 After Douglas dies, which of these things do you think Cosette will do?
   a continue her safe life.
   b change her lifestyle completely.
   c invite the story-teller to live with her.

While you read

9 Complete this description of the story-teller.

Name ....

Job ....

Where she lives ....

Oldest friend ....

10 Underline the fact that is wrong about each of these people.

   a Bell never reads books, she lives with a painter and has two children.

   b Felicity and Esmond live at Thornham Hall, they are Elizabeth's relations and they have a lot of parties.

   c Silas Sanger is a painter, lives in a cottage with Miranda and drinks a lot of alcohol.

   d Cosette is interested in Elizabeth's story, is moving to Notting Hill and has bought a house with 106 stairs.

After you read

11 Work with two other students. Act out these interviews.

   Student A: You are a detective. You want to find out about Silas's death. Ask Bell and Felicity questions.

   Student B: You are Bell. Answer the detective's questions.

   Student C: You are Felicity. Answer the questions.

Chapters 6–8

Before you read

12 Look at the picture on page 12. It is the 1960s when Cosette moves to Notting Hill. This time in London was called the Swinging Sixties. What do you know about life for young people at this time – the hair, the clothes, the music? Talk to other students.

While you read

13 Look at these pairs of events. Which event happens first in each pair? Write 1 and 2.

   a ..... Felicity phones Elizabeth with Bell's phone number.

   ..... Cosette starts to wear bright colours and changes her hair.

b ..... Elizabeth has to wait two or three years to discover if she
has inherited Huntington's Chorea.

..... Her mother shows the first sign of the illness when she is
thirty-six.

c ..... Elizabeth meets Bell again.

..... Cosette finds Ivor Sitwell in the park with a young girl.

d ..... Elizabeth goes to Florence with Cosette.

..... Elizabeth hangs a painting by Bronzini in her study.

e ..... Elizabeth starts to write her first novel on Cosette's old
typewriter.

..... Bell is living in a simple room with a bed, a table and a
chair.

After you read

14 Answer these questions.

  a What is Cosette's main aim in life when she moves to Notting
  Hill?

  b Why is it too late for Elizabeth to have a blood test for
  Huntington's Chorea?

  c Is Ivor Sitwell in love with Cosette?

  d Why doesn't Bell have a job?

  e Where did her money come from?

  f How does Elizabeth feel when Bell phones her after all this
  time?

  g When Bell disappears, she knows all about Elizabeth. What
  does Elizabeth know about Bell?

Chapters 9–11

Before you read

15 How much do we know about Bell? Make notes and then
compare them with other students' notes.

While you read

16 Are these sentences right (✓) or wrong (✗)?

  a Elizabeth and Bell meet again by chance at the
  theatre.   .....

b Elizabeth wants to meet Bell's brother Mark.   .....

c Bell kisses Elizabeth.   .....

d Elizabeth believes what Bell tells her about her past.   .....

e Bell asks Cosette if she can have a room in the
House of Stairs.   .....

f Bell dresses exactly as Lucrezia Panciatichi.   .....

g Elizabeth and Bell become lovers.   .....

h Bell went to prison for killing Silas.   .....

After you read

17 Work with another student. Have this conversation.

Student A: You are coming to live at the House of Stairs. Cosette
is showing you round. Ask lots of questions.

Student B: You are Cosette. You are showing a new lodger
around the House of Stairs. Show him/her all the
rooms. Describe what life is like there.

Chapters 12–13

Before you read

18 Think about these questions.

a Why does the writer talk about the bloodstone so often?

b Who is Susan and what happened to her, do you think?

c Will Milly Theale be important in Bell's story? Why (not)?

While you read

19 Underline the wrong words in these sentences. Write the right
word in the space.

a Bell's feelings for Elizabeth are getting
stronger.   ....

b Cosette is looking very attractive when
Mark visits for the first time.   ....

c Bell is afraid that Mark will break
Cosette's heart.   ....

d Bell says that her parents sent her
away to school when she was sixteen.   ....

e Mark stayed the night after Bell's
  birthday party. ....
f Bell once loved Elizabeth. ....
g As Mark and Cosette become closer,
  Bell and Elizabeth become closer. ....

After you read

20 Complete this description of Mark.

Mark is Bell's older **(a)** … . He is an **(b)** … and he works in
(c) … . His skin and hair are **(d)** … than Bell's. He isn't **(e)** … and
he is very **(f)** … . He tells Elizabeth that he thinks Cosette is a
(g) … person.

Chapters 14–15

Before you read

21 How do we know Elizabeth is getting Huntington's disease?

While you read

22 Put these sentences in the correct order. Number them 1 to 10.
  a ..... Bell goes to Thornham for Christmas.
  b ..... Bell realizes something has gone wrong.
  c ..... Cosette and Mark want to move to a little house.
  d ..... Cosette is suddenly very rich.
  e ..... Elsa comes to stay.
  f ..... Mark doesn't want to marry Cosette.
  g ..... Mark drives out most of the lodgers.
  h ..... Mark and Cosette sleep together.
  i ..... Mark loses his job.
  j ..... Mark moves in to the House of Stairs.

After you read

23 Bell asks to see Mark privately. What do they talk about? Talk to
other students and write down your ideas. When you finish the
book, see if you were right.

Chapters 16–17

Before you read

24 Look at the picture and read the words on page 42.
  a Who is this woman, do you think?
  b Who are the people around the table?

While you read

25 Who might say these things? And who to? Write the names.
  a 'Why do you have so few things?'

    .... to ....
  b 'I'm not going to help you lie to Bell.'

    .... to ....
  c 'What a surprise! How lovely to see you!'

    .... to ....
  d 'Come and meet your brother's friends.'

    .... to ....
  e 'Is there something wrong with the food?'

    .... to ....
  f 'I can't believe I didn't know they were lovers.'

    .... to ....
  g 'I forgive you.'

    .... to ....
  h 'It's all your fault. I never want to see you again.'

    .... to ....
  i 'I don't want to lose Cosette. She's a mother to me.'

    .... to ....

After you read

26 Which of these characters do you feel most sorry for? Why?
  a Bell   **b** Cosette   **c** Elizabeth

Chapter 18

Before you read

27 Chapter 18 is called 'Murder'. Discuss these questions.
  a Who is going to be murdered?
  b Who will the murderer be?

28 Underline the correct words in *italics*.

    a Elizabeth *has/hasn't* spoken to Cosette since Bell went to prison.

    b Mark was afraid of *Bell/Cosette*.

    c Bell *knew/didn't know* that Mark was going to marry Cosette.

    d Bell *knew/didn't know* that Mark really loved Cosette.

    e Bell *was sorry/felt great* as soon as she had pushed Mark out of the window.

    f *The police/Cosette's brother* took Cosette away.

    g Bell's younger sister was called *Sheila/Susan*.

    h Bell murdered *two/three* people.

    i Bell got all her ideas from *Mark/Elizabeth*.

After you read

29 What do you think of the ending? Talk to other students.

Writing

30 At the end of the story the telephone rings. Elizabeth goes to answer it. Continue the story. Who is on the phone? What do they say? What happens next?

31 At the end of Chapter 18, Elizabeth writes to Cosette (see page 53). What does she say? Write her letter.

32 Douglas has died and Cosette has left Hampstead. She has started her new life in Notting Hill. She writes a letter to a friend in Italy. She describes the changes in her life. Write her letter.

33 Look at a copy of Bronzino's painting of Lucrezia Panciatichi (on the internet). Write a description of Lucrezia.

34 Choose one of the pictures in the book. Describe what is happening, what has just happened and what is about to happen.

35 You are a police detective. You visited the House of Stairs after Mark was killed. You interviewed everyone who was in the house at the time – Cosette, Elsa and Elizabeth. Write your police report. Say what you are planning to do.

36 You are Bell's lawyer at Bell's trial. Bell says she is guilty of the crime but you want to get a shorter sentence for her. You can argue that Susan's death and Mark's death were accidents. (Nobody talked about Silas's death at her trial – see page 24.) Write your speech. Try to give good reasons for Bell's behaviour.

37 A property company is selling the House of Stairs after Mark's death. Possible buyers know that a murder happened here. Write a description of the house for buyers. Be positive!

38 After the disastrous meal at the restaurant, Mark tells Cosette almost everything about him and Bell (see pages 45–6). Write their conversation.

39 Find out about London in the 1960s. Find out about life for young people then. Write about some of these things: the politics, the music, the lifestyle, the clothes, the shops and the parties.

WORD LIST

aloud (adv) spoken, not silently

betray (v) to be disloyal to someone who believes you will be loyal

bloodstone (n) a dark green stone with red spots

cancer (n) a very serious disease

cheek (n) the soft round part of your face below each of your eyes

children's home (n) a place for children whose parents have died or cannot look after them

cottage (n) a small house, often old, in the country

delight (n) a feeling of great pleasure and satisfaction

divorce (v) to officially end a marriage

dove (n) a white bird, often used as a sign of peace

extremely (adv) very

freedom (n) the ability to do what you want without people stopping you

hairdresser (n) a person who cuts and styles people's hair

heroine (n) the woman or girl who is the main character in a story

hippy (n) a person, especially in the 1960s, who had long hair, wore unusual flowery clothes and believed in peace

inherit (v) to receive money and/or property from someone after they have died

lifestyle (n) the way a person chooses to live

lodger (n) a person who pays for a room in someone's house

nod (v) to move your head up and down to mean 'Yes'

novel (n) a long written story which is fictional

obvious (adj) very easy to notice or understand

relation (n) a relative

roulette (n) a game in which a small ball is dropped onto a moving wheel with 36 numbers on it, and people try to win money by guessing which number the ball will stop on

savings (n) all the money that you have saved, especially in a bank

sister-in-law (n) the sister of your husband/wife, or the wife of your brother

somehow (adv) in some way, or by some method, although you do not know how

telegram (n) a short written message sent electronically, which was common before the invention of more modern methods

trial (n) the situation when a court of law listens to information about a crime and decides whether a person is guilty or not

typewriter (n) a machine with keys that you press in order to print letters onto paper

will (n) a legal document that says who you want to have your money and property after you die